Who's in the Egg?

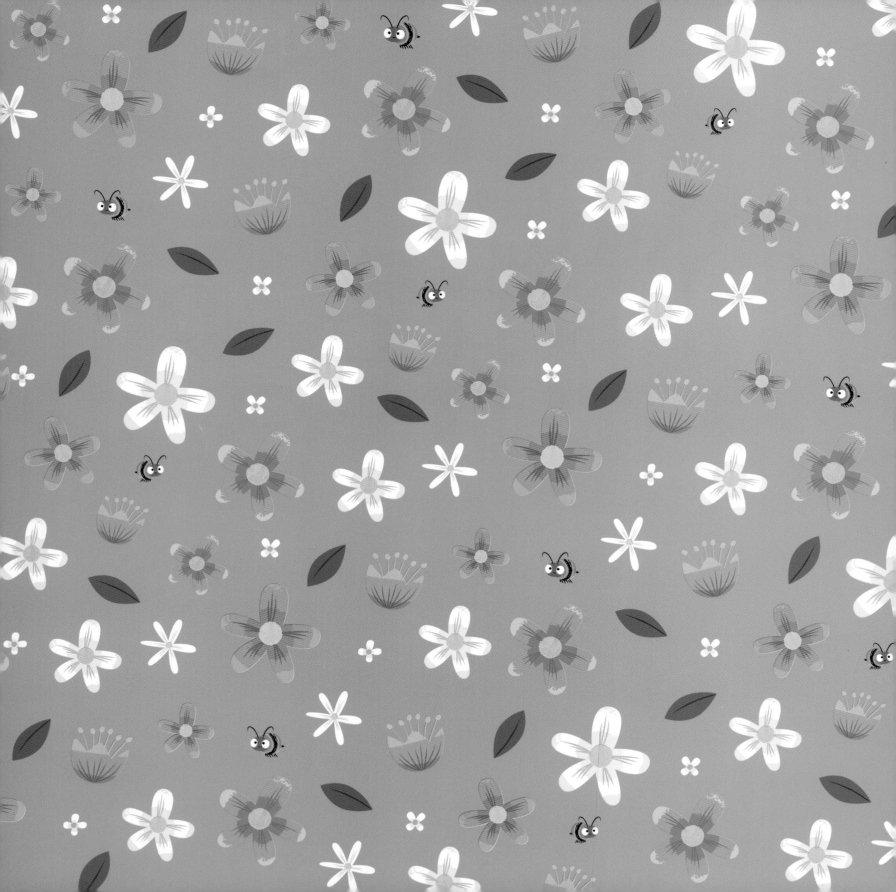

Can you spot this egg on every page?

First published in Great Britain in 2020 by Pat-a-Cake
This paperback edition published in 2022

1 3 5 7 9 10 8 6 4 2

Text by Pat-a-Cake • Illustrated by Dean Gray • ISBN: 978 1 52638 374 7
A CIP catalogue record for this book is available from the British Library
Printed and bound in China

Pat-a-Cake, an imprint of Hachette Children's Group,
Part of Hodder & Stoughton Limited
Carmelite House, 50 Victoria Embankment, London EC4Y 0DZ
EU address: 8 Castlecourt, Castleknock, Dublin 15, Ireland

An Hachette UK Company
www.hachette.co.uk • www.hachettechildrens.co.uk

Who's in the Egg?

Illustrated by Dean Gray

It's time for Mummy Hen's chick to hatch,
but she can't find her egg!

Is it that one by the lake?

Who's in the egg?

Mummy Hen is still looking for her egg.

Is it that one out in the snow?

Who's in the egg?

It's a baby penguin!

"I'm not your chick!"

Mummy Hen is STILL looking for her egg.

Is it this one on the river bank?

Who's in the egg?

"I'm your baby chick.

I love you,

Mummy!"

Can you match the pairs?